Ink and Embers

Kamalika Bhattacharya

Ukiyoto Publishing

All global publishing rights are held by

Ukiyoto Publishing

Published in 2024

Content Copyright © Kamalika Bhattacharya

ISBN 9789362693242

All rights reserved.
No part of this publication may be reproduced, transmitted, or stored in a retrieval system, in any form by any means, electronic, mechanical, photocopying, recording or otherwise, without the prior permission of the publisher.

The moral rights of the author have been asserted.

This is a work of fiction. Names, characters, businesses, places, events, locales, and incidents are either the products of the author's imagination or used in a fictitious manner. Any resemblance to actual persons, living or dead, or actual events is purely coincidental.

This book is sold subject to the condition that it shall not by way of trade or otherwise, be lent, resold, hired out or otherwise circulated, without the publisher's prior consent, in any form of binding or cover other than that in which it is published.

www.ukiyoto.com

Dedication

Sharing the heartbreaks, ups and downs, joys and sorrows is an entirely new experience. I frequently get choked up when I think about the misery that individuals endure. I appreciate everyone who helped me depict my stories, poems and concepts. I would like to express my gratitude to my family for continuing to support me as I complete my task. Mom, I appreciate how you always smooth out the edges of my imperfections. I appreciate you encouraging me to persevere no matter what. Although I mourn you, Dad, I still draw inspiration from you in all of my writing.

Contents

Ripples	1
Timeless Edge	3
Heartbeats	5
Timequaint	7
Concealed	9
Wordshore	11
Undying Love	13
Infinite Solitude	15
Reflection	17
Treasure	18
By the Sea	19
Winter	21
Escape	23
The Unwritten Pact	25
Unspoken Verses	26
Unscramble love	28
Intimacy	30
Spot it!	32
Heart string	34
Encircle	36
Quake of thoughts	38
Entrapped	40
Blur	42
Hidden Gem	44
A dream comb	45
Moonlit Curse	46
About the Author	*48*

Ripples

I dismiss the fairytales and myth,
Everything I won't be able to say
Yet believed it all,
I know where you belong.

To reach you is a coveted journey,
When I told my heart a million times not to fall for you,
For my heart was scared of yet another disaster.
And my heart belongs to you and I dismantled all my feelings to discover the most important one: YOU.

I hope to find a kind of love that
makes the sunrise brighter for us,
I hope to see my missing piece once again,
When your wild heart won't be afraid to embracethe love that would make the sunset softer.

The fairytales have limits, but love is never ending,
You're entwined in my mind and soul innately, My heart won't ever trade you for anything,
I won't need another hand to hold mine,
Because, I will fail to understand and reciprocate
As I do to you.
Love is not tangible,
I remember the way I smiled on my way back home,The day I confessed my love to you,
Like a fistful of gold dust sparkled my eyes,

Although a thought of you pierces my heart,
And yet bring solace at once,
I wish you could understand, how much I miss you
In a way that would make your heart ache as mine.

Timeless Edge

A spark of feelings that dwell
Beneath your skin and rushes
through your veins,
That stimulates your actions,
Good or bad, vibrant or dull,
Helps you to evolve.
A truth that no one wishes to accept,
A secret everyone likes to guard,
made of millions of unsaid words,
some known, and some unknown.

Fire too brings a spark,
But it's powerful than the flames, For
it ignites your soul deep within, In a
moment it electrifies your mood,
in yet another you drown yourself in silence,
True spark never burns the other,
It doesnot vapourise,
A process that remains unchanged.Irreversible.

On the contrary, you find your solace inA river
that twists and flows consistently back to the
sea,
It just flows…
For certain things are beyond give and take,

Just a mere need to reciprocate,
To unearth the hidden feelings
Of the heart,
Longings, not subjective but deeper than that,
A flow of thought, a flow of current,
We carry for each other,
No one to blame,
No one to slander,
Just in search of each other,
And become timeless.

Heartbeats

Love has nothing to do with what you are expecting.It
is about what you are ready to offer irretrievably.
Those million moments when I want you,
While knowing it all that I must wait.

The emotions become restless and my soul like a
fluttering bird
Caught behind a silver cage,
Thinking about all that mere words could endure,
Thousands of emotions strike at one go,
The ebb of silence floats,
Deep down I know, without you
Everything is meaningless,
Everything loses its charm,
It's you, always you.

The essence of love, and with this I can repaint and
restructure everything at my disposal,
Renew my canvas with hope,
Strengthen my core with care,
Take small little steps one at a time,
To stimulate growth.

I overcome the pain of accepting your absence,
Sometimes by letting go and sometimes by holding
on to it,
The wear and tear of emotion harbours
In the corner of my eyes,
The resistance to share my thoughts with you
sometimes is part of my battle to learn

the language of my heartbeats, Missing
you is just not another phrase, It's
deeper than it appears.

It's a saga on my way to learn
To seal the stolen moments in the deck,
While embracing the solitude,
And curating pleasure amidst this
Confusing pain that aches my heart
Like never before.

Timequaint

She is a canvas of poetry and pain, She
has thousands of unspoken tales,But
she has a few takers
Who could see the depth of her soul,
When she was kind,
She was not appreciated and was disdained,She
had warmth in her eyes,
to look at the social miseries.

And yet continue to being kind to the people
Who manipulated her, devasted her core,
ripped off her gentle soul,
Made her what she is today.
She battled the yearning of being accepted,
For who she is.

She could not disregard her soul any longer.She
pulled herself out,
from the waves of their endless talks,
Which meant nothing but added extra scars toher
soul,
she deserved someone unequivocally committed,
who would not filter the words nor slam her for
anything,
someone who would give her wings to be free,Yes!!
there will be void around her,
but she deserves peace,
she deserves love,
let her grief remain concealed beneath a smile, She
has a heart filled with love and unsaid words,

Let the vacuum collapse,
Because,
In this materialistic world,
A grab on his hands is the only treasure,She possesses.

Concealed

Within every being there is a
Healer, a warrior, a leader, A
divine self.
Disrespect is the last resort
Of a relationship.

Each tear that rolls down,
Acts as a punctuation in the process of healing,
Countless nights robbed off sleep
entails the chapters of the tormented heart,
that we forbade to encounter.

There is never a ritualistic closure,
We all need to know that we start to heal
only when we recognize true love for ourselves.Yes!!
There is nothing greater than love,
And we need to absorb that in abundance,
there is a doorway from heart...
After all the closure is the ultimate narrative.

We seek peace, more than anything.
In the beauty of allowing the closure,
I secretly invite the beauty of making poems,
Of all those unsaid emotions, a silent dance inside
the hollows of my chest...
I wished to experience a closure,
Not to anchor and wad my heart experiences.Just
peace.

Some insightful words to refurbish our soul,But
never bargain with the soul,
And its quotient of happiness.

Because that is the only thing you broughtAnd
you can take back.
In the process of healing when your
Eyes become moist,
Know that tears will be a mode of prayers,
They travel far and beyond
When our words are frozen
And we seek closure and peace.
The key of all our happiness
lies in prayer.

Wordshore

I want to grew up as a kind hearted person,
With sheer good intentions and no
Expectations,
With less of anxiety, and more of divinity,
With less of blockage and more of forbearance. With
less of disapproval and more of solicitousness.With
less of hurt and more of gentleness.
With less of barbarousness and more of
thoughtfulness.

With less of selfishness and more of graciousness.
With less of harshness and more of tolerance,
With less of cruelty and more of affection.
With less of disadvantage and more of benevolence.With
less of meanness and more of charity.

With less of obstruction and more of magnanimity.With
less of hindrance and more of clemancy.
With less of hostility and more of acceptance. With
less of indecency and more of beneficence.With less
of animosity and more of tenderness.

With less of injury and more of succor.
With less of pride and more of amiability.
With less of resentment and more of assistance.
With less of prejudice and more of helpfulness.

With less of impasse and more of considerations.
With less of foulness and more of goodness.
With less of outrageousness and more of indulgence.
With less of coarseness and more of altruism.
With less of vileness and more of temperance.

With less of offense and more of endurance.
With less of greed and more of qualm.
With less of malice and more of regard.
With less of beastliness and more of compassion.

With less of covetousness and more of agreement.
With less of wickedness and more of responsiveness.
With less of pettiness and more of warmheartedness.
With less of unworthiness and more of affinity.

With less of apathy and more of generosity.
With less of detachment and more of bounty
With less of listlessness and more of forgiveness.
With less of disdain and more of humanity.
With undivided love and unparalleled feelings

Let's grow in eachother, for eachother.

Undying Love

My man won't ride a white horse,
I don't believe that he has to bring the moon
to propose me,
I won't need his luxury machine to offer me a ride,I
won't expect him to have the royal palace at his
disposal,
I won't need a super expensive holiday every year
To prove his love for me,
I won't need him to stretch himself to get me
the biggest solitaire around my finger,
I won't look for those extravagant parties every time,I
would love to see him,
enflame my heart and fill my spirit with those fluttering
butterflies, by walking that extra mile for meensuring of
my smile.

I need someone, who would
romance my mind, uncover my soul.
A passionate heart who's willing to strike the rightchord
of the heart and keep all the overblown egos and
superficial
desires aside for once, just to smile with a simple
wink.

Just to discover my source of happiness. He
will never fall short of reasons to love,
He would be able to read my heart's loose ends,
Under all circumstances, he would be ready to claim
my soul with his reckless pursuits.

A simple cottage with a small bunch of flower garden
hanging by the kitchen window,
A playlist that will entail the unspoken words and
Charm our emotions once again to fall for eachother,
A not so perfect dance, when he would see the
depth of my kohl smugged eyes,

And never miss a chance to give a peck onmy
high check bones…
He would always swear by my alluring gaze. A
random drive and a quick stopover by an Ice-
cream parlour,

My man would taste my words with deep anticipation,
Waiting for each syllable that would melt his
Desires slowly and steadily,
His mind would race and quickens with an urge to
Pervade my solitude,
As each day awakens,
All I will ever need is

A promise that
Whatever life brings us, we won't
Give up, even if it rains down that sought
To tear us apart.
Forever until time is no more.

Infinite Solitude

There is a pathless shore before me,
There is a wide horizon that is endless,
There is an unknown trail of deep forest that
beckons,
There is a vast path drenched in moonlight,
The picture of mine that reflected in your eyes,Is
what I have and will always admire.

The last thought as I fall asleep with, each night
And the first smile as I rise each morning, with a hopeOf
you being there somewhere,
Transform my energies to sail through the roughnessa
tiring day brings.

The birds chirp and flower blooms,
The wind blows and that ember sky looms,
A day filled with challenge and a night
That is long and cold,
Having a tender heart,
Am withering inside and
Wish your palms in mine to hold.

The battle of love is unknown to all,
Some claim it as divine,
Some terribly fall,
Deep down I keep everything to my heart,Hoping
things won't fall apart,
Your candid smile is eloquent and lush,I
think of us, when voices inside me
Makes me hush,
Into a trail of a relinquished dreams,

Underline by the echoes of a trembling heart,I wish we could meet once ,
Beneath the safest chambers of your heart.
Moon and me, You and I
are merely a dream,
untimely paired,
yet brings me a gleam.

Reflection

The day i gave up on the very thought,
Not to think twice, and abandon my heart.
You bumped on to me again,
And I looked deep into your eyes.
My instinct were, I was taken,
I had surrendered long time back,
Even before I confessed the truth,
But never told you the turmoil of my heart
And smiled with an excuse.

There were millions of thoughts,
Thousands of emotions floating
across my eyes, I wished only once,if
you could have looked into
them and realized the perplex
layers of a heart that admires you selflessly.
Nothing could ever have been
simple and nice than feeling
Love is the only component
That comes without notice and
consumes the most of us,
And also helps you to flourish.

The day I confessed , I wore a smile
That out shined my flaws and
brought sparkle to my eyes,
I learnt to peep into yours
With an exciting intrigue.

Treasure

Words of mine, may find a way to reach your heart, I
would like to stay right there, where mine belongs to,
And what would you do,
if you knew what my heart yearns to hear?
Would you let those syllables turn into a
colour blast or a riddle to tickle my senses?

Would you let those words slip into me, Say
i have waited too long,
Yearning for those trembling lips
of yours to hold my name between them,
Longed badly enough to stare at that
blank wall and imagine you holding me against it,
Untill my eyes brim and tears come rushing by,
And you run your fingers through
 my hair caressing,

Till my breath is choppy and yours melting in mine.
The butterfly kiss by your lashes on my cheek
bones that rushes down a sweet urge to
hold you close for a few moments,
And those moments are my treasure.
Trapped into the bones…

As unclaimed treasure.

By the Sea

The sea shore that I knew
Had two perspectives,
One having a quiet beam visited by
The waves to fill it with life,
As per the clock,
roaring and yet gently bobble down,
while the sun beams get to write
those unsaid verses of their love
Across the waves.

The rimless wave tracks are witness
Of bounty and bliss.
The other being too busy and bustling
It might reach all those who loved.
Visited more by people and a little less
by those coquette waves who
Were afraid of reaching out
And plunk down happiness
And absorb the stillness
concealed between the chaos.

She appeared like a sea,
Bustling with energy,
Rushing with her arms open,
Only for a reason that
electrifies her emotions,
Laced with the
sweetness of love.

That day unlike putting
her stern brave face her coyness took over,Her
heart softened.
Lapped towards his body, with an urge to planta
gentle kiss,
She leaned onto him,
Drenched herself in all his being.

Captured with intense warmth,
That moment was everything,
The beautiful and a blissful one,
Lasted only for a few moment though,
She withdrew. And returned to herself,
And she remained
On the shore...
Awaiting love and peace.

Winter

With every particle of me,
With all the emotions I feel,
With all the air I breathe,
In silent hope that
You will sign on with a smile
Expressing the brilliant metaphor,
That bridges the two soul,
Longed enough for each other,
For being a refuge in your arms.

The eloquent connect we
Could establish stands by the
Charm of love that blinds us
In the colloquial world,
That denies emotional
Hurricanes and believes
That spring is waiting.

Even though the heart
That trembles in fear,
Anxiousness wants to
explore the warmth
That two hearts generates,
Because it's winter.

The stained eyelids that made the
pillowcase the witness of all that it feels.
The Untold grief, the undiscovered scars,
Amid these never ending sunset,
Each day bringing new shades,

A journey through the shadows,
Facing the fear, deepest emotions,
And yet holding onto the faith
Of being a steady anchor for each other
Could be the only precious gift we
Bring to the table besides
everything.

Escape

Let this poem take us back to the
Memory lane,
When love was not
a kiss or a touch,
But being fragile in
each other's ears,
Let's begin again.

Let's fall in love with
each other's core,
The undiscovered scars,
the untold grief,
The unwoven dreams,
the fears, the darkness,
The flaws.
Everything.
That makes us beautiful,complete.

No lukewarm feelings, but that strong desire,
Willingness to admire and love completely only
By accepting and healing each other.
My heart is a place where both love
and longing share a bed,
where i touch your absence every day
and yet caresses it with gentleness..
Without you there is a hollow space
that won't ever be filled inside me...
You my darling heart...
plunge into my heart casually, to
understand the tides of love.

May you know that
You are not amazing in a way
like a single rose petal is,
you are amazing in a way a garden is...
Amidst all emotional hurricanes,
you are my anchor.

The Unwritten Pact

When I fail to manipulate on the feelings,
that rushes down my spine to convince
My worth.
Our love being superior is
the only thing between us,
Let this remain the acknowledgment of
Our love tale...
May this unwritten pact of
Love be the only thing
we could give and take from each other.
The assurance of being there, no matter what,
Just recognising the values of commitment
That is embeded in my essence,
I would want you to know that
I don't engage casually.

When am in, it's my profound trust
That could fade away all the flaws
We have and beyond.
I just seek reciprocal value,
Let honesty be our currency.
Am not ashamed of being so selective to give
access to only a few people
into my life, for finding a person Worth
of your love is an extraordinary
Experience.

You being that sunshine,
Makes our love tale unique.

Unspoken Verses

In the creases of your palms,I
have seen the landscape.
I always dream to have,
And that deep ocean that
takes shelter behind your eyes,
Are chambers that would
Bring me solace.

The marks of old scars on your
skin are mere sparkles,
Oh! I could see mirrors even in your freckles,
When you smile those lines of your face
Brings me joy and assures that
Facial intonations are priceless
And exclusive too,
They hold stories in each crease.

You belong to my heart even
when you don't even care to tell me
how it feels for you to absorb this love,
your heart is clueless to express
how it feels on being kissed…..
i discovered this not in one go
but travelled and suffered
enough to realise a small little reaon
That kindles my heart-
my Home is within you…

I never thought twice to call you,
my home even when you made me
wait for that one silly call to tell

The magical verse " i love you".
You say, you can hear me through silence.

If so, hear those unspoken verses
soaked in love and
what i spoke only to you
even when i was quiet for all...

Impart the memories that will seepin
my bones, And that my love
would be precious than that of jewels, if any…

Unscramble love

May my heart always find excuses to fall in love
with you again and again...
Inside the darkness and serenity of midnight'sstill..when
you hold the door ajar
as i step into the world without you.
Yet it remains you.

When i return home on a tired evening,
Just to get enveloped in your arms,
When you leave my hands and walk away, In
anger, in fear and sometimes just like thatMy
heart trembles as if a part of me got
distraughted and the rest screams at you in silence
For leaving me in awe.

When i wrap my arms around the soft pillow
just to feel if i could hear that heartbeat of yours,
And the tears soak the pillowcase slowly,
When i fight with youjust
to tell you i care,
When you scold me firmly
and yet i could feel your love,
When you tremble and subside
to complete me,
I regain all my power and feel
rejuvenated.
I await you in the daylight and
even in those darkest midnight

to unscramble me
like the moonlight illuminates
the bank of that dark river,
And the water reflects back
Nothing but light,
Bejewel me with your silver touch.

Let the shimmer on my skin
Radiates nothing but sweetache,
And while the stars stare down in wonder,And
those unconscionable fear.
Does the hoofed dance on my brow,
Know it's both a blessing,
and a curse to feel things so deeply...
**Feels so innately, and yet being able to
Unscramble the word called Love.**

Intimacy

Intimacy is about safety!! Isn't it?
Peace you feel in someone's presence...
The ease in voice when you disagree,
Someone's attentiveness
when you are struggling.
Their tone when they speak,
to you and about you...

The urge to discover your core,
yearning to love you even when words
become incapable to communicate, no
matter what...
I loved you the way i found you
under various circumstances.
Happy, sad,delighted, silent, withdrawn,
open, laughing with tears in the corner of your eyes,tired,
excited, emotional, confidante,
straight,brave, trying to fix me and my emotionsand
everything that is you.
I didn't fancy for a perfect you.

I too have uncountable flaws.
I always wanted a subtle real you, who
would be able to shed off the
burden and will find happiness in
my embrace, in the small little things
that makes you and me - US.
I smile when you express your

love even when your voice shakes
and you summarise everything
unspoken to "miss you"
Love isn't abstract,
i see it in you. Undeniable.
By loving you, all i have
done so far is
walking down a road
resonating with my souls
scream,because for me You matter.

Spot it!

You are the laughter that
echoes in the corridors of my heart,
In the silence of nights,
when i ride the chariots.
Of yesterdays,
I am crowded by your memories,
That distinct fragrance of yours.
My fingers still remembers the
meadows of your face,
Those timeless curves of your lips,
And that tranquillity of
Your face...

Listen my love,
I want to remember you,
Long after the silverfish
would have eaten my youthfulness,I
want to recall your face,
the spark of your eyes,
the echoes of your voice
calling out my name,
the crook of your arms,
the Clasp of your hands on mine,
The arch of your dreams, i barged into,
The butterflies of our first kiss,
The turbulance of my heart
When i surrendered,

The light of that moment
when we became US,
The wet pillowcases and
my trembling lips
Uttering your name,
The pain of the tattoo
inking our love,

A gaze of yours meeting mine,
Those silent pillow talks we shared,
Those lazy moments
in each others arms,
Those bundle of love
we know we have,
Those colours of sorrow
we always hide,
That parting of hands
when we said goodbye,
I want to remember you,
A little longer than,
Your memory allows you to.
Just spot it and keep it
Safe.

Heart string

When our silence speaks and
We touch each other, the longing of
ours out pours and feels more
than static on the skin,
Silk and skin feels the same,
You recess so perfectly in me,
As my arms drape over your side.

As if you are a known
Predisposition from time unknown,
Woven in my DNA perfectly blended.I
wonder we were alien once,
And never expected that we were
Would mean so much to each other.

Our hands clasped with each other,
And when feet intertwinedwithout
any coordination,
yet when they settle when we tangle ourselves inlove,
They want a ground that can shelter Us.
Winter slowly glides into the spring,
When i find myself in your embrace,
So close that i could easily
Hear your heartbeats,
Your breaths as warm as sun's beam of rays,
Comforts my soul inadvertently.
You are my kingdom, my randomness,
My uniqueness, my pride,

My being flourishes when i realise,
You are my rock,
My everlasting plan.

Encircle

What if I die suddenly?
Won't I be able to escape all
The banishment, pain, slander!
That came my way!!

It crosses my mind often,
But my fear of losing you
Succumbs my spirit,
What if there is no light
The other side,
I would wait for you, even in darkness.
where shadows wait for a light,
Where fallen leaves return to reborn,
But what if am forbidden,
What if there is no return,
What if there are no stars
That allows me to talk to you,
What if you fail to recognise my soul,
And I will have to wait again..
A long wait,
What if you give up on me,
Just because I will be gone,
Will that be defeat of my love,
Or will that be defeat of my soul?

Everything will encircle again?
Will everything begin again?
Or will you escape me,
You see, they say,
We shouldn't claim in love,

We should just surrender
And allow love to
Dictate us forever,
But, when everything
Appears to encircle and
Strike us back,
It sends a shiver down my spine,
For love consumes us,
A bit of us in a better way.

In love, we find our home in a
Person, while we are on the shoresTo
share our encircling pain
That balms our emptiness.

Quake of thoughts

The world says, time is a great healer,It
heals the wounds of the heart, And
the scars that our soul carries.

Sometimes its the trauma,
The heart catches up with,
The fear and pain of losing you,
That muted everything,
I didn't know, i am yet
to feel the collision.

Just like how winter slipped away,
To the lap of spring.
Much like how old friends converse
and try to know everything that is
hidden within, slowly with a pause.

I was yet to restructure my life always,
Thinking i have enough and more time
To sit down and talk to you.

You as usual would have thought
about it much in advance,
for you have been my
Best advisor,
Not someone who forced me
to something,
Not someone who questions
my likes and dislikes, not someone
who judged me so often and

made my walk confident.

Therefore, much before i
could hold you and say
thank you,much before i could say,
"there were many things
i did and many i didn't"
just because of you.
Because "you matter, always and more"

A state of grief arrived on my doorstep,
Much like how waves lash on the shores, to
offer the pain, i was not ready to handle,
Somewhat like when you're
unwilling to plunge, because you are already,
Struggling within,
The grief stricken waves, has the power
To sink ships, and your departure was"
the end " to many things
known and unknown.

Entrapped

Looking across the wide horizon,
It strikes me more than often to ask you this:
"Is there a place for me in the courtyard of your heart?"
While you filled the chambers of my heart
with the vibe of yearning,
i never wanted anything from you but you....

The devils doing a hoofed dance
Over my head strikes me with curiosity
Whether you are tied up with genuine
Emotions towards me or
Are you going with a flow,
Just because you are not aware how to stop,my heart devoured in love,
the pearls, the rubies, the fig tree of my soul..

The seeds of love, the scars, the worries, the dreams
everything leads to you.
Distance taught me to live
Without you and yet yearning deeply for you.
The deadly dilemma, that keeps me enchanted
And freaked out at the same time.

How could i endure this life without
revealing my universe to you…
Adjusting the odds is given,

I don't expect you to fix anything for me…
I've learned to fight my battles,
But there are times a soilder too needs.
a blessed hand to recover from the hardships,
Those moments I look for you, want you by me.…I
am too scared to expect anything but,
With the promise of yours to recreate our love tale,i
row the boat of my dreams to the harbour of your
soul…
You are that unique bond,
unscripted and unplanned love tale,i
never want to part with..
When i miss you terribly,
I wonder who i yearn for so eagerly,
Is it you or the piece of me that left with you…
I just hope we don't lose each other in
the forest of small little things…

Blur

When love knocks your door,
it doesn't care for any excuses.
Love never would abandon you,
when you need it the most.
Love doesn't look at you to
say you ask for too much.
Love surfaces.

It make all the efforts
For that one person against all odds.
Crosses boundaries,
Breaks rules and yet is as
spontaneous as wind that blows
As swift as river that flows,
In the urge to meet the ocean.

Love brings along intimacy,
To state your goofy self around them.
being vulnerable, admitting your fears,
Being honest and upfront
about what you want.
Just being able to bare
Yourself to someone is
Incredible and the only responsible
Element is love.

Oh love!! Kill me in your embrace..
Then revive me again with a kiss everyday.

Don't leave me without your gentleness
and your intimacy..
Burn me with your sun and hide me.
Under this moonlight such
wonderful deep could be insightful
love. We embrace it unknowingly
and keep in the safest chamber of our heart.

Known to all yet unknown to many...
I have cried my heart out, what a sea it is..Once
you fall in love,
you know what a trouble it is,
what fulfillment this is...
What endurance this is...

Let me stay warm burning in the flames
for this is what my heart longs for...
My heart still struggles to take your name
without a slur, yet my insomnia
allows me to picture you without a blur....

Hidden Gem

I am jealous of your eyes,
Not by the way they seem to be,
But, the way they shine and sparkle
with childlike charm,
Ever wonder how they hold stories
And hide secrets,
I am yet to know.

I wish i could be that confidant,
With whom you would share,
Only if i could see through,
those eyes for a day and more.

I won't mind diving into them
to discover the untold pain and
hidden heartaches,
So, what if was not a witness to all
Of it but, sharing the pain
Would gives unimaginable pleasure.

Discovering each and every layers of
You would be rewarding,
And someday,
I would be able to command you,
Those eyes shall never be moist
With lace of sadness, Ever again.

A dream comb

When he uses words her eyes speaks,The
language not known to all,
Everytime ours met,
I felt the current,
The secret pact between us,
Between us!! when there is
something overwhelming,
and we hesitate to cross our
gaze even for a moment.

Eyelids flutter to speak,
Yet in silence they
know what to say,
He lifts his,
Mine fall.

And when i look at him,
He puts them down,
That fluttering of lashes
upon our cheeks,
gives us thousands of
those butterfly kisses...

With silent confessions,
In the language of
Eyes.
When eyes speak,
words don't interfere.

Moonlit Curse

A powerful and magnificent symbol
Of light and beauty,
That white disc. The moon.
One that hangs out, diminishes everyday,
washed away by the clouds,
Overshadowed by the ever burning
Sun.Transforms every night and
yet continues to dazzle.

Whenever i look at the moon,
it feels like you too somewhere
are doing the same.
Looking at it, talking and sharing
Everything that troubles our heart.
And it listens as if
It possess the power to heal.
constructing a magical link to the sky,It
tries to bridge the gap in silence.

We're miles apart and often
feel abandoned,
Can we afford meeting on the moon?
Picture us laughing,our words floating
in the moonlit place.
Shed those fears and perhaps the moon
Would give us our new address.
A place where distance won't matter,
silence won't feel heavy,

words will float...And our dreams will
expand… from nothing to something
And from something to everything.
Of being true to the emotion that is
imprinted in our souls fabric for each other.

A place where you won't
shy away to hold me close.
A place where you won't have to
weigh your words and speak.
I want to hear those verses that you often keep locked
beneath the safest chamber of your heart.
May the spell of love break
the spell of moonlit curse.

About the Author

Kamalika Bhattacharya

Kamalika Bhattacharya has written poems, short stories, and editorials for a variety of publications. Her work skillfully blends passion, drama, and love. Her work skillfully blends passion, drama, and love. Books: Smitten by Love. Sacred Scoop. Who's your forever? Threads of fate, etc.

www.ingramcontent.com/pod-product-compliance
Lightning Source LLC
LaVergne TN
LVHW041554070526
838199LV00046B/1963